SOME SWAHILI WORDS

Chewa
he who has a very large mouth

Choyo
greed

Kiboko
hippopotamus

Leo
today

Mbili
two

Mega
worn down

Moja
one

Ngawa
civet cat

Sarabi
mirage

Tatu
three

Wali
cooked rice

THE
LION KING

VULTURE SHOCK

by Judy Katschke

Illustrations by Laureen Burger
Brooks & Rachelle Campbell
Denise Shimabukuro

Produced by Mega-Books, Inc. Design and art direction by
Michaelis/Carpelis Design Assoc., Inc.
Printed in the United States of America.

Grolier Books

ISBN: 0-7172-8350-X

CHAPTER

1

"Kopa!" Nala called to her cub. "Where are you off to now?"

"To the water hole, Mom." Kopa's tail was twitching. "The antelopes are having a fight. Dad's gonna break it up."

"Must you follow your father everywhere?" asked Nala.

"Sure!" answered Kopa. He puffed out his chest. "There's a lot I have to learn if I'm gonna be king someday."

"Like hunting for your own supper?"

"Hunting?" cried Kopa. "Mo-om! That's girl stuff!"

"Sorry, Your Majesty!" Nala laughed

as Kopa scurried away.

Kopa was the son of Nala and Simba, the Lion King. When Simba was young, his father, Mufasa, had been killed. Thinking that his father's death was his fault, Simba had run away. Simba did not know that Mufasa had been killed by his evil brother, Scar. It wasn't long before Scar became the Lion King.

Simba lived far away in the jungle until his old friend Nala found him. Nala persuaded Simba to return to the Pride Lands and take his rightful place as king.

Simba defeated Scar and became the new Lion King. Later, Simba and Nala became mates and the parents of a lively cub, whom they named Kopa.

"Wait till I tell the other lions about the antelope brawl!" Kopa knew where to find them.

The pride was resting under a clump of acacia trees. Kopa ran to greet them. They did not notice him.

"Did I ever tell you about the time my

great-grandfather chased a herd of elephants?" asked Leo.

"About a hundred times!" said Boga.
The other lions groaned.

Ngawa, a civet, peered from behind a
bush. "The way I heard it, Leo"—he
grinned—"it was the elephants who
chased your great-grandfather!"

Leo fumed. "In fact," Ngawa said, "I
heard they weren't elephants but mice!"

"Oh, yeah?" growled Leo.

"Hey, guys!" Kopa called. "My dad—"

"Get real, Leo!" said Sabini. "What
you want is Simba's family tree, and
you'll never have it."

Kopa's ears perked up.

"Hmmmph. My family tree is even
better than Simba's!" Leo sniffed. He
turned to Kopa. "No offense, kid."

"No family tree is better than
Simba's!" said Sabini.

"What family tree?" asked Kopa.
"Where is it?"

The lions laughed.

"Is it big?" asked Kopa, his eyes widening. "Does it have a lot of leaves? What kind of fruit grows on it?"

The lions were rolling on the ground.

Kopa puffed out his chest. "Stop laughing!" he said. "Tell me where my family tree is!"

Kopa stared at the lions. "Come on, you guys! Please?"

Mega, an old lion with a full mane, said, "Your father would want the honor of telling you about your family tree."

"You're right," Kopa smiled. "I'm gonna ask him right now."

The lions watched Kopa dash away.

"'Does it have leaves?' he asks." Babu giggled. "'Or fruit?'"

"Cubs!" Ngawa chuckled. "They say the darndest things!"

"Which reminds me," said Leo "Did I ever tell you about the time my great-grandfather saved a cub from a—"

"About a hundred times, Leo!" cried Sabini.

CHAPTER

"Who speaks for the antelopes here?" asked Simba.

Nzee stepped forward. "It's like this, Simba," she said. "We love our water hole. It's cool. It's fresh. And it's clear."

"But?" asked Simba.

"But we can't drink with that slob Kiboko in it!"

"Hey!" called Kiboko. "Who says this water hole is yours? I don't see your name on it."

He swung his head sideways, spraying them with water.

"You see what I mean, Simba?" cried

Nzee. "He's humongous, he's filthy, and he stinks!"

"Yeah! And proud of it!" called Kiboko.

Simba looked at the antelopes. "You realize that hippos like the water too?"

"Why does he have to like our water?" asked the biggest antelope, Machufa.

"Kiboko? What was wrong with your swamp?" Simba asked.

Kiboko rolled in the water lazily. "I guess you could say my tastes have changed." He took a gulp of water and gargled loudly.

"That does it! Let me at him! Let me at him!" screamed Nzee.

Kopa squeezed his way through the crowd of antelopes. "Hi, Dad!" Kopa called. "Got a minute?"

"Kopa!" said Simba. "This isn't the place for a cub!"

"Dad!" cried Kopa. "Tell me about our family tree! The lions were talking about our family tree. I want to find it!"

Simba smiled. "Find it?"

"Yeah!" said Kopa. "I want to find it and climb it and—"

"Simba!" called Nzee. "What about Kiboko?"

Machufa came forward. "Do we have to get ugly?"

Kopa tugged at his father with one of his claws. "Da-ad! Can I climb the family tree? Can I? Can I? Huh?"

Simba looked down at Kopa, then at the antelopes.

"Go ahead!" Kiboko grinned. "Make my day!" He began to swing his head sideways again.

"Kopa!" Simba said. "Later!"

"Simba! Simba! Simba!" chanted the antelopes.

Kopa backed away from the water hole. "I don't need anyone to help me find the family tree," he whispered, "because I'm going to find it myself!"

CHAPTER

The antelope squabble was only half settled. All that Kiboko had agreed to do was wash his feet before entering the water hole.

I don't know what's harder, thought Simba as he walked home, being king or being a father!

"Rough day, sire?"

Simba looked up and saw the hornbill Zazu, his steward. "Let's just say I was up to my neck in work, Zazu."

"Oh, dear!" Zazu sighed. "It's a good thing you're not a giraffe!"

"Zazu, was I curious when I was a cub?" Simba asked.

"Hmmmm. I do recall an incident many years ago," said Zazu. "One regarding an elephant graveyard—"

"Never mind!" The elephant graveyard still made his mane stand on end.

"Why do you ask, sire?"

Simba sighed. "Kopa wants me to tell him all about our family tree. And I don't know where to begin."

Zazu said, "Well, sire, you can start by showing him this."

"What?" asked Simba.

"It's a surprise, sire," Zazu said. "Follow me."

Simba hadn't realized that Zazu's surprise was so far away. They traveled for an hour over grassland and along the Zuberi River.

"Zazu!" Simba called. "Where are you taking me?"

Zazu flew toward some bushes. Simba watched as Zazu cleared the mouth of a cave by brushing aside the branches with his beak. "Enter!" said Zazu.

Simba gasped when he walked into the cave. Lines were scratched all over the wall. One line led to another, then another and another, like a tree with many branches.

"Sire," Zazu said with a sweep of his wing. "May I present your family tree!"

"Fantastic!" cried Simba.

"Look, sire. This line stands for your father, the noble King Mufasa. It is joined to another line, Sarabi, your mother," Zazu said with a salute.

"And the line next to Mufasa is—"

"Your uncle," Zazu sneered. "That slime-bucket Scar."

"Why have I never seen this before?" Simba asked.

"Because you never asked."

Simba turned to see Rafiki, bowing at the mouth of the cave. He gave the old baboon a big smile.

"*Asante sana*. Thank you very much, Rafiki," he said. "Wait till Kopa sees this!"

"Speaking of Kopa, sire," asked Zazu, "where is he now?"

Kopa had wandered down Pride Rock to the grassy plain below. The land looked strange, and many of the bushes were taller than he was.

"Don't ever go beyond the Pride Lands alone!" his father had warned him.

But what if our great family tree is out there? Kopa wondered.

A beetle scuttled toward a hole.

"I really should grab something to eat," Kopa said, stretching out his claws.

A lizard popped its head out of the hole, scaring away the beetle.

"Hey!" Kopa yelled. "What do you think you're doing?"

"Just digging the scene!"

Kopa stared at the lizard. It was a lot bigger than the beetle.

Kopa's stomach growled.

"Lion, plus growling stomach, plus me—equals lizard lasagna!" said the lizard. "Look, I'd really love to stay for dinner," he said. "But I've gotta run!"

Kopa watched the lizard dash out of the hole and scurry away.

"I'm gonna get you!" cried Kopa.

He chased the lizard for what seemed like two hours. The high grass had turned to dust under Kopa's tired paws when the lizard finally disappeared.

"Those hunting lessons of Mom's are looking awfully good," he said and dropped to the ground. "I give up!" It had grown dark. "Gosh! Where am I?"

The ground was dry and broken. Dead trees were everywhere. They looked like claws.

"I'm Kopa," he mumbled, "I'm a prince. And I'm not scared of anything!"

He stepped forward and felt something under his paw. He looked down and saw a skull. It stared up at him with hollow eyes.

CHAPTER 4

"Well"—he shuddered—"almost anything!"

Kopa settled himself under a dead tree. He listened to the strange sounds that filled the night.

"I want to go home," Kopa whispered. The chilly air made him shiver. He curled up and cried himself to sleep.

"What do you want to eat today, Chewa?"

"I don't know. What do you want to eat today, Choyo?"

"I don't know. What do you want to

eat today, Chewa?"

"I don't know— Darn! We go through this every day!" cried Chewa. He was a vulture and was talking to his friend Choyo. "What difference does it make when there's nothing to eat?"

The vultures stood silently on a rock. They watched the sun coming up over the dry, dead land.

"It's just not the same anymore." Choyo sighed. "Animals aren't migrating the way they used to."

"And when they don't migrate, they don't get lost," added Chewa. "And when they don't get lost, they don't drop dead. And when they don't drop dead, we don't eat!"

"That's why you're the leader of the flock, Chewa. You're so smart!" cried Choyo.

"Let's face it, Choyo, my friend," Chewa sighed. "It's either beast or famine. And as your leader, I can do nothing about it."

"Remember the good old days when Scar was king?" asked Choyo. "We had animals passing through every day."

"Ah, yes! I can taste it now." Chewa's beak trembled. "Antelope antipasto! Bush-baby bouillabaisse! Polecat Provençale!"

"Jellied jackal!" added Choyo. "Ginger-glazed gazelle! Miniature warthog puffs!"

The two vultures jumped off the rock. They touched wings and began dancing in a circle.

"Rib roast of rhino! Giraffe gazpacho!" They danced around a dead tree.

"Coconut crème cub!" said Choyo.

"Cub?" shrieked Chewa. Sleeping a few feet away was Kopa.

Chewa grabbed Choyo by the wings. "It's a lion cub!" he screeched. "Do you remember the last time we ate lion cub?"

"I can't remember the last time we ate anything!" wailed Choyo.

"Exactly my point," said Chewa.

"This little kitty is going to make our tummies tingle!"

"Hey! We can't eat him yet." Choyo lifted Kopa's eyelid. "He's not dead!"

"Choyo, we may be birds of prey," said Chewa, "but we are not creatures of habit."

"No?" Choyo said. "No! Of course not."

"Besides"—Chewa sniffed Kopa—"I certainly could acquire a taste for fresh, chubby cubby feet."

"So what are we waiting for?" asked Choyo.

Chewa knocked Choyo over with his wing. "Choyo! Have you already forgotten the main rule of the flock?"

"We have rules?" asked Choyo.

"Rule number one: Whatever we find, we share," said Chewa.

At the word *share*, a dozen more vultures swooped down from the sky.

"Baby cub!" cried one.

"Tasty!" cried another.

Back at Pride Rock, Simba and Nala were pacing the ground.

"It was my fault," Simba said. "I shouldn't have been too busy for Kopa."

"Don't blame yourself, Simba," said Nala. "It was my fault. I should have kept him from wandering off."

"No!" cried Zazu. "It was my fault. I should have seen him going."

"It was my fault." Rafiki sighed. "I should have seen it coming."

"Oh, let's stop blaming ourselves," Zazu said.

They turned to see Kiboko. He was covered with mud and flies—but his feet were clean.

Zazu pointed his wing at Kiboko. "It was his fault!"

Fast asleep, Kopa did not hear Chewa, Choyo, and the new arrivals. Curled up next to the tree, he snored softly as the vultures eyed him.

"Before we dine, I would like to make a toast," said Chewa.

"Speech! Speech! Speech!" called the vultures.

Chewa raised his wings modestly. "May we never need five hundred ways to prepare crickets again!"

"Hear, hear!"

Kopa yawned. The vultures jumped back when he rolled over. Their beaks quivered as they watched him stretch.

"What do you say, Chewa?" asked Wali, an eager vulture. "Do we eat him alone or on a bed of wild mice?"

"Wait!" cried Chewa. He walked over to Kopa and stared into his face. "Don't you get the feeling you've seen this cub before?"

"Only in my dreams, Chewa!" shouted Choyo.

"Yeah!" said Wali, clacking his beak. "This here is one royal feast!"

"Did you say *royal*?" cried Chewa. "That's it!"

"What?" shrieked Choyo.

"This cub is the son of Simba, the Lion King! Which makes him the prince of the Pride!"

"Who cares?" Wali said. "In the stomach, they're all the same!"

"This little cub is not going into anyone's stomach," said Chewa.

"You mean we're not going to eat him?" cried Choyo.

"No!" said Chewa. He leaned over Kopa, who was just opening his eyes.

"With a father like Simba," Chewa said, "there's a lot more to be gained from this measly little cub. A lot more. Wah-ha-ha!"

CHAPTER 5

et me down!" Kopa shouted.

"Aw, don't you like your new tower, Prince?" called Wali.

Kopa's new tower was a spiky nest of twigs resting on top of a tall, dead tree. The tree was far too tall and smooth for a little cub to climb down.

"I'm hungry!" cried Kopa. The vultures laughed and flew away.

Kopa buried his head in his paws. "Why can't I be brave like my dad?"

"Hey, chill out, little brother!"

Kopa looked up. Three young vultures were standing around his nest.

"Who are you?" gasped Kopa.

The vultures put their wings around one another.

"I'm Moja!" said the first.

"Mbili!" said the second.

"Tatu!" said the third.

"Better known as—ta-da!—the Buzzard Boyz!" they shouted together.

"The Buzzard Boyz?" Kopa asked.

Moja, Mbili, and Tatu began beating on the nest with their wings.

"Hey!" cried Kopa. "What are you—?"

"Just listen to the word of the bird!" said Tatu. The vultures sang:

"We're the Buzzard Boyz,
And you know our wings are flappin'!
We're not like other vultures,
'Cause we'd rather be here rappin'!"

The buzzards folded their wings across their chests.

"That was great!" said Kopa.

"Don't jive us, man!" said Moja.

"No! That was way-cool!"

The vultures exchanged high fives.

"That's the first time we've heard that," said Mbili.

"Don't the other vultures like your music?" asked Kopa.

"Let's put it this way," said Tatu. "When we're hummin', they're bummin'!"

"Sorry to hear that," said Kopa.

"That's why Chewa would rather have us up here with you than down there with him," said Moja.

"What's he going to do?" Kopa gulped. "Eat me?"

"No, man!" cried Tatu. "Chewa wants to make a ransom deal with your dad!"

"You, in exchange for a bigger, fatter, tastier creature," added Moja.

"And if Daddy isn't cool," continued Tatu, "then we have the ugly task of—"

"You know, guys," Kopa said, "I'd really love to hear another song."

"Bust the move, Boyz!" cried Tatu.

"Yo! Sometimes we prey on ostrich,
We always swoop to catch 'em!
But when they lay their eggs,
We do our best to hatch 'em!
Check it out!"

"Awesome!" cried Kopa. "Wicked awesome!"

"Singin' for a prince!" cried Moja. "Man, this is def!"

"I'd like to hear more," said Kopa. "But my stomach is growling too loudly to hear anything!"

"Man, let's get the cub some grub!" said Tatu.

The Buzzard Boyz flew off.

Whew! thought Kopa. That was a smart move!

Then Kopa smiled. Maybe I'm more like my dad than I thought!

CHAPTER 6

Surrounded by his flock, Chewa sat on a rhinoceros skull. He rubbed his wings together. "Now, we all know that Simba will do anything to get his dear cub back. Don't be afraid to think big!"

The vultures sat in silence.

"Oh, come on!" cried Chewa. "Don't we even have a wish list?"

Choyo raised his wing. "I'd like to exchange the cub for three dik-diks."

"Out of all the animals in the Pride Lands, you come up with dik-diks?" cried Chewa. "The tiniest antelopes in Africa!"

"I meant three big antelopes," said

Choyo. "Light but satisfying."

"Antelope!" Chewa sniffed. "I would rather eat a cantaloupe than an antelope!"

The vultures chuckled politely.

"Now," continued Chewa, "shall we try it again?"

Another vulture raised her wing.

"Ye-ess?" asked Chewa.

"How's about we exchange the kid for a waterbuck?"

Chewa sighed, "We already discussed the appetizer."

"How about a wildebeest?" asked another vulture.

Chewa rolled his eyes. "Please, sir! Can I have some more?"

"Well, what do *you* want to eat, Chewa?" asked Choyo.

"Yeah! Yeah!" the vultures shouted.

Chewa did a little dance.

"If I had to choose one meal, it would be elephant!"

"Yes!" cried the vultures.

"Or hippopotamus!"

"Yes! Yes!" cried the vultures.

"Or rhinoceros!"

"Yes! Yes! Yes!"

"Wait! Wait! Wait!" cried Chewa. "Why settle for one dish? Let's give Simba a menu of the animals we want."

"Are you sure we're not asking for too much, Chewa?" asked Choyo.

"Of course not, my dear friend," said Chewa. "After all, greed is good for us!"

The Buzzard Boyz stood in the back of the crowd. They shook their heads.

"Vultures eating live animals?" whispered Tatu. "That's not cool!"

"That bird is out of control!" said Mbili.

"Way out!" Moja whistled softly.

"What d'ya say, Boyz?" asked Tatu.

"I say this time we don't follow the leader!" murmured Mbili.

"Right on!" whispered Moja.

"Now," Chewa said, "do we all agree on the curried cream of crocodile with crispy croutons?"

CHAPTER 7

"You mean they want to eat all those animals?" Kopa gasped.

The Buzzard Boyz had returned to the nest. They chanted:

"Chewa's got a menu,
The list reads like a zoo!
The deal is really simple:
It's the menu or it's you!"

"My dad will never let those vultures hurt the animals in the Pride Lands," said Kopa. "And I don't blame him!"

"Yo, man!" cried Moja. "Cool your whiskers!"

"You're right, I don't want to get eaten," Kopa whispered. "But Dad can't sacrifice the other animals for me!"

"Well, he may not have to," said Tatu. "Wait till you hear our plan."

"Plan? What plan?"

"See you later!" The Buzzard Boyz flew off.

"You want to *what?*" cried Chewa.

"We want to deliver the menu to Simba," said Tatu.

"Yeah!" said Mbili. "The Buzzard Boyz want to hang with the king!"

"The fat cat!" cried Moja.

"The mane man!" cried Tatu.

"No!" Chewa said, shaking his head. "Choyo is going to deliver the menu. And that's that!"

Choyo stuck his beak in the air. "And that's that!"

"Too bad, man!" Tatu sighed. "We had ten new songs to sing for Simba."

"But if we can't sing for the leader of

the Pride . . ." continued Moja.

"We'll have to sing for the leader of the flock!" cried Mbili.

"Songs?" Chewa gulped. "Ten songs?"

"Check 'em out!" cried Moja.

The vultures began to sing:

"Yo! The Buzzard Boys are fly!
We know we're number one!
So get the party pumpin',
'Cause we've only just begun!
Go, Chewa! Go, Chewa!"

They took a deep breath.

"Hold it!" cried Chewa, clapping his wings over his ears. "No more!"

"We can't help it, man!" Tatu smiled. "We're culture vultures!"

"Well, now you're messengers!" snapped Chewa.

"What?" squealed Moja happily.

"But, Chewa," cried Choyo, "I was supposed—"

"Shut your beak!" Chewa screeched at

Choyo. He turned to the Buzzard Boyz. "Wali will tell you everything that is on the menu," he said. "Memorize it and recite it for Simba. But do not—I repeat—do not tell him where the cub is! Do you hear me?"

"We hear you!" chanted the Boyz.

"Chewa, why the Buzzard Boyz?" asked Choyo.

Chewa pulled Choyo aside. "Because once those annoying creatures open their beaks," he whispered, "Simba will agree to anything!"

Chewa marched over to the Boyz.

"Go find Wali," said Chewa with a salute. "And may the course be with you!"

"Don't worry, Chewa," said Tatu. "As soon as the spread is in the head, we'll make a beeline for the feline!"

"Come on, Boyz!" Moja called. The Buzzard Boyz flew off.

"Now, why would we ever tell Simba where the cub is"—Tatu laughed—"if we can sing about it instead?"

"I'm glad we're helpin' the little dude," said Mbili. "He's nice, cute—"

"And he's got great taste in music!" said Moja.

In the Pride Lands, tears flowed heavier than Zulu Falls. The animals gathered on Pride Rock to comfort Simba and Nala. Even Kiboko and the antelopes forgot their squabble to help find Kopa.

"A search party!" cried Zazu. "We must form a search party!"

"Quickly! Before it's too late!" cried Nala. "My baby is probably starving! And thirsty! And watched by hungry vultures!"

"Speaking of vultures," cried Kiboko, "look!"

The Buzzard Boyz were circling above.

"Vultures!" cried Leo.

The animals cleared the runway as the

vultures touched down one at a time.

"Smooth landing!" Tatu smiled and dusted off his wings.

"Who are you?" asked Simba.

"Man, we thought you'd never ask!" Moja smiled. "Go with the flow, Boyz."

The Buzzard Boyz began to sing:

"If you were hopin'
For canaries,
Be wary—
'Cause we're slammin'
And we're jammin'
And we're hopin' and we're wishin'
For an end to our famine—"

"Stop!" Zazu stepped forward. "We are not in the mood for a recital!"

"But you will be in the mood for this!" said Tatu. The Buzzard Boyz continued to sing:

"We're the Buzzard Boyz,
And we're here to get things done,
Like lead you where you need
To go to find your son!
Word of the bird."

"Sire!" cried Zazu. "They know where to find Kopa!"

"Tell us where he is!" Nala cried.

"It's not that easy!" Tatu sighed.

"What do you mean?" Simba snapped.

The Buzzard Boyz folded their wings across their chests. They began to sing:

"Our leader's name is Chewa.
He wants to make a deal.
He'll give you back the cub
If you whip him up a meal!"

"A meal?" Simba asked. "What meal?"

"Whatever it is," cried Leo, "just do it! Do it!"

"It's like this, Simba, my man," explained Moja. "Chewa wants to exchange Kopa for some larger animals."

"On the other hand"—Leo gulped—"you might want to give it some thought."

"Exchange my son," Simba said, "for my friends? I can't do that!"

Kiboko broke through the crowd.

"Send me, Simba!" he shouted. "I can handle them!"

"What a guy!" cried Nzee.

"Thank you, Kiboko," Simba said. "But that creature seems to want more than one animal."

"You got that right!" said Tatu. "Check out the menu!"

"Menu?" Simba asked. "What menu?"

The Buzzard Boyz cleared their throats. "The first course consists of a mongoose salad with slivered snake!"

"Oh, no!" cried a mongoose.

"Sssssay it ain't sssso!" hissed a snake.

"Followed by a plate of hyena hash with *huevos rancheros*!" said Mbili.

The hyenas were not laughing.

"Followed by an old-fashioned gazelle gumbo," said Tatu.

A gazelle fainted, barely missing Zazu as she collapsed.

"You don't happen to have hornbill on the menu . . . do you?" Zazu gulped.

A herd of elephants joined trunks and began dancing in a circle. "They don't want to eat us! They don't want to eat us!" they sang.

"Don't get excited!" said Tatu. "You boys are the entree!"

The elephants stopped dancing.

"Would you care to hear the specials?" Tatu asked politely.

"No animal here is going to be eaten!" Simba marched over to the Buzzard Boyz. He growled. "Are you going to tell me where Kopa is, or do I have to get fierce?"

The Buzzard Boyz stepped back.

"Sorry, man! But we're not allowed to tell you," Tatu said.

"Chewa's rules." Moja shrugged.

"Oh, really?" Nala snarled at the Buzzard Boyz.

"But we've got nothing to lose . . . if we sing you the news," Mbili said.

"Then sing!" Simba cried.

"Bring it home, Boyz!" cried Mbili.

"The cub is bummin' in a nest
On top of some dead trees
Where the breeze is hot and dusty
And all you do is sneeze!"

Simba's eyes widened. "Huh?"

Rafiki grabbed a stick. He began drawing in the dirt. "Dead trees . . . dusty breeze . . . all you do is sneeze . . .."

"Rafiki!" cried Nala. "Do you know where it is?"

Rafiki stared down at his drawing. A drawing of a dead, spiky tree. Rafiki nodded. "Follow me!"

The animals cheered.

"Now, how did he find out?" asked Tatu.

"I have no idea!" Moja smiled.

"It's not like we told anyone where he was." Mbili winked.

The sun had set, and the air grew cool. Kopa tossed in his nest of twigs.

What if the Buzzard Boyz' plan doesn't work? Kopa thought with a shudder.

A vulture cackled below.

"Good night, Sweet Prince!"

Kopa stuck his head out over the twigs. He opened his mouth. "Roarrrr!!"

Hmm, thought Kopa as he watched the vulture scurry away. Not bad!

CHAPTER

The sun came up the next day and shone on the vultures.

Chewa was sitting on the rhinoceros skull, staring out at the desert.

"Hey!" cried Choyo. "I'm hungry!"

"Idiot!" snapped Chewa. "So am I."

"Where are those Buzzard Boyz anyway?" called one of the other vultures.

Chewa shrugged. "Can I help it if the food is good but the service is only fair?"

"Chewa?" Choyo asked. "How does an elephant smell?"

Chewa rolled his eyes. "With his trunk. What a riot."

"No, Chewa!" said Choyo. "I think I

smell an elephant. And a jackal. Look!"

The Buzzard Boyz soared over a hill. They were leading a parade of animals.

Chewa jumped up. "Ladies and gentlemen, dinner is served!"

"Yaaaaaaay!" cried the vultures.

The sound of the marching animals woke Kopa. He peeked over the edge of the nest and rubbed his eyes. There was Rafiki! And Zazu! And Kiboko! And the antelopes!

"Wow!" he whispered. "What a turnout!"

The sound of the animals' tramping was so loud, Kopa covered his ears.

"It's—it's a smorgasbord!" Chewa cried. "A beak-smacking smorgasbord!"

The parade of animals stopped in front of the skull.

"Chewa, my man!" said Tatu. "We proudly present the zoo plate special!"

The vultures gasped as they looked over the animals. "Aaaaaaaaaah!"

"It's perfect!" Choyo sobbed.

Chewa jumped down from the skull. "No! It's not!"

"It's not?" said Choyo.

"I see the hors d'oeuvres, the appetizer, the soup, but no dessert!"

"Picky, picky, picky!" Mbili sighed.

Chewa stamped his foot. "A fine meal like this calls for dessert! Where's the dessert?"

"Chill your bill, man!" said Tatu."It's right next to the giraffe gazpacho."

Chewa walked toward the giraffes.

"If I remember correctly," said Chewa, "the menu called for flamingo flambé!"

The Buzzard Boyz huddled together, whispering. "We've replaced the flamingo with another well-known animal. Will he notice? Let's watch and see!"

Chewa walked past a giraffe. He stopped next to Kiboko.

"Who are you?" Chewa asked.

Kiboko smiled. "I'm your dessert!"

Simba and Nala jumped out from behind Kiboko. "And we're your worst nightmare!" Simba growled.

Choyo's feathers stood straight up.

"You know what?" Chewa gulped and ran. "I think I'll skip dessert!"

"Oh, no, you don't!" Simba grabbed Chewa by the wing.

"Where's Kopa?" snarled Nala.

"Kopa?" asked Chewa. "I don't know a Kopa!" He turned to Choyo. "Do you know a Kopa?"

"N-no Kopa here!" said Choyo.

"Hey, Mom! Dad!"

"Kopa!" cried Nala.

"Where are you?" Simba called.

Chewa dashed behind the skull.

"Oh, that Kopa," he chattered nervously. "We have so many guests, I lose track!"

Simba stared into Chewa's eyes.

"Wait!" cried Chewa. "You can take back your brat—I mean, son. But we're so hungry. Can't we take a bite out of just one of those animals?"

"Which one?" asked Simba.

"Oh, like that wimpy little hornbill!" said Chewa. "He can't possibly mean anything to you!"

"Zazu just happens to be my trusted steward and friend!" roared Simba.

Chewa stared at Zazu.

"On the other hand"—Chewa gulped—"everything looks so good. What do you suggest?"

The animals surrounded Chewa.

"I hear vulture vichyssoise is excellent!" grunted Kiboko.

"A-ahhhh!!" Chewa screamed.

Choyo marched over to Simba and Nala. "Hey! This is our wasteland! You can't just come here and turn everything upside down!"

"You mean, like this?" asked Nala. She grabbed Choyo by the foot and began shaking him.

"Arrrrrgh!" screamed Choyo. Nala dropped Choyo on the ground with a thump.

Simba put a paw on the rhinoceros

skull and glared at the other vultures.

"May I suggest that you birds return to your old eating habits?"

"No problem!"

"The deader the better!"

"Love those rats!"

Simba turned to Chewa and stared into his eyes.

"Don't bite my head off!" Chewa cried. "Please!"

"Don't worry!" Simba growled. "I have a more suitable sentence in mind!"

"What's that?" Chewa shivered.

"You and your friend Choyo are hearby ordered to attend a concert once a week."

"How lovely!" Chewa smiled with relief.

"A Buzzard Boyz concert!"

"The Buzzard Boyz?" Chewa shrieked. "No! Anything but the Buzzard Boyz!"

"You and your stupid menu!" Choyo hissed at Chewa.

"And we'll be checking up on all you

vultures," said Nala, "to make sure that you never break the laws of nature again!"

"Man!" Tatu smiled. "These cats are bad!"

Rafiki climbed the tree and brought Kopa down.

"Mom! Dad!" cried Kopa. He nuzzled his mother happily.

"I'm so glad you're safe!" cried Nala.

"I'm sorry I ran away," said Kopa.

"I'm sorry I didn't listen to you." Simba licked the top of Kopa's head.

The Buzzard Boyz began to sob.

"I can't take it, man!" wailed Tatu.

"They're breakin' my heart!" bawled Moja.

"These family reunions kill me!" sobbed Mbili.

Simba and Nala walked over to the Buzzard Boyz.

"Thank you for all you did." Simba smiled and looked at Kopa fondly.

"Please visit the Pride Lands whenever you can," Nala said.

"Yeah!" Kopa grinned. "You guys got the slammin'est sound ever!"

"*Slammin'est*," Zazu repeated. "I suppose that means 'good.'"

Kopa jumped on Simba's back.

"Mom! Dad!" he cried. "I was up in a tree! A dead, spiky tree! Do you want to hear all about it?"

"As I recall, you wanted to talk about another tree," said Simba. "Our family tree."

"Cool!" cried Kopa.

"You see," said Simba, "a family tree isn't really a tree, but a record of our family. It has everyone's name on it, all the way back to our noble great-great-great-grandparents!"

Simba looked over at Rafiki and winked.

Kopa waved good-bye to the Buzzard Boyz. The parade of animals set off on the journey back to Pride Rock.

"I'm gonna miss the little dude," Mbili sighed and waved back at Kopa.

"What do we do now?" asked Moja.

"We pump it up, Boyz!" cried Tatu.

"Oh, no!" Chewa moaned.

The Buzzard Boyz strutted around Chewa and Choyo. They began to sing:

"It don't matter if you're a buzzard
Or a lizard
Or a tiger
Or a mole or a mule
Or a hippo or a gecko
Or an orphaned chimpanzee.
There's something we've all got,
And that's a family tree!
Word of the bird."